A LONG LONG SONG

ETIENNE DELESSERT

For Reb

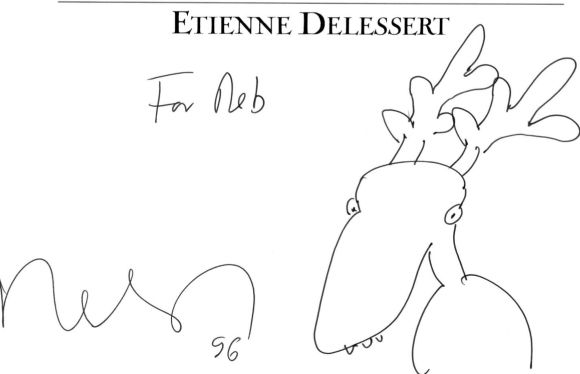

96

MICHAEL DI CAPUA BOOKS
FARRAR, STRAUS & GIROUX
NEW YORK

FOR MY FATHER
1889–1960

As I was going along, long, long,
A-singing a comical song, song, song

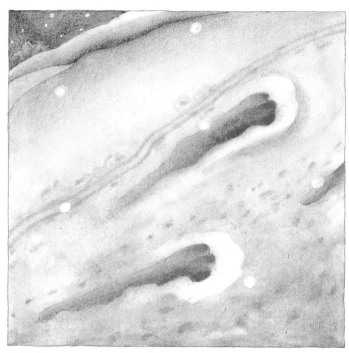

The lane that I went was so long, long, long

And the song that I sung was so long, long, long

And so I went singing along